名流詩叢 34

紅雪
The Red Snow

雪白茫茫落下
潔白覆蓋一切山脈
雪也白茫茫落下
庫德斯坦山脈
但立刻血紅一片

〔庫德斯坦〕 胡塞殷・哈巴實 (Hussein Habash) ◎著
李魁賢 (Lee Kuei-shien) ◎譯

【序】詩是愛 *Poetry is LOVE*

　　我說詩就是愛，愛就是詩，二者可在稱為地球的美麗行星上生存。詩消弭人與人之間的距離，在心靈間契合，透示深埋在人心中之美。沒有詩，生活會變得暗淡、沉重、無法忍受。詩解脫我們，不致怠惰、艱苦，讓愛情鳥在人生的綠枝上，快樂幸福鳴唱。深感台灣詩和庫德詩好像雙胞胎，受苦受難的孿生子，也同樣處在愛和希望中。感謝我的偉大朋友和台灣詩人李魁賢，把我一些詩翻譯成漢語普通話。感謝詩……詩萬歲！

胡塞殷・哈巴實

庫德斯坦

目次

❶ 紅雪

雪白茫茫落下

潔白覆蓋一切山脈

雪也白茫茫落下

庫德斯坦山脈

但立刻血紅一片

❷ 正好知道我死了

要是有一天你來找不到我

正好知道我死了

要是你來那裡找不到我

正好知道我在遠地

要是你到遠方找不到我

不要傷心

在大地深心裡種一株紅玫瑰

知道我死了！

❸ 愛情之用

大家都知道地球是圓的
不懷疑會轉動
但沒人知道
情人的心是怎麼變圓的
而愛情的力量
怎麼轉動。

❹ 兩棵樹相愛

兩棵樹瘋狂相愛

懷恨的伐木工

砍斷樹幹

帶回家

兩棵樹在火場偶然相遇

很高興擁抱

一起焚燒。

譯自 Muna Zinati 英譯本

❺ 來日你總是會老

（對我來說，多多少少在四分之一世紀內）

來日你總是會老

柺杖始終與你同在

你會孤獨走路

會像所有怪老子一樣自言自語

變得頑固，不聽人言，動作遲鈍

你需要時，就會求助

卻無人理會

你會夢見過去

良好舊時光

而你的孫子則會想到未來

和即將到來的日子

你會咒罵這個無趣的世代

像破裂的唱盤一再重複

我們世代多麼美妙

你會成為家裡開玩笑的對象

他們會取笑你

和你認為是正確的立場

你的嘴唇會露出嘲弄微笑

每當他們提到像固執、

精力充沛和對未來有信心等字樣

你甚至可能笑到

骨頭軟掉

疾病會在你體內自由漫遊

不需經過許可

你的所有慾望都會消失無蹤

除了想要死掉

將會沒有朋友或伴侶

孤獨將是你的支援和同志

你將永遠準備離開

墳墓的門檻將誘惑你，與你同在

所有的天使會棄你離去

只有死亡天使會接近你成為最後朋友

也許你會說，就像你準備離開：

如果我死了，把我埋在此地無主公墓

也許這些話

將是你的最後願望。

❻ 貝多芬和庫德人

我凝視貝多芬的身影

他看來悲傷

庫德人群

按照他們步驟檢查市中心

沒什麼大不了的事，除了渴望

貝多芬哭泣

我凝視萊茵河

把城市劈成兩半

顯得悲傷

是為幼發拉底河悲傷嗎？

幼發拉底是悲傷

❼ 母親的聖詠

1 幻象之歌

今早，母親獨自坐在家裡

縫補哥哥馬哈茂德

昨天頑皮撕破的褲子

針刺到手指，溫暖的血流到線上

染到褲子，母親心思不寧

今早她看到我或我的影子

或者看見我沒有影子在她面前走過

就罵我父親和鄰居

她看到我的時候

迷迷糊糊中急於擁抱我

可是針反叛她，刺到她手指

真的是我在

還是母親的心在那裡？

2 渴望之歌

母親，

三十年了，我還在赤腳奔波

每當我看到女人穿長裙

或頭上的白色圍巾

我會叫她：母親，母親

母親啊！

三十年加六千英里

逃亡離開玫瑰、旭出、天使的臉，

母親的臉

三十年

每當我寫到女人

每當我畫女人

我發現自己在寫我母親

用我母親的色彩給形象著裝

三十件壽衣，三十座墳墓，三十個……

我用希望和平靜心處理

就像我的頭

擱在媽媽的胸口。

3 熱情之歌

我們土造房屋牆壁塗鴉

門上黃漆

細心掛在伊瑪目阿里旁邊的家族照片

烤箱馬口鐵皮的敲擊痕跡

門邊安靜的大石頭

都隨時準備接待客人

貨架堆滿舊報紙

燈以發光的長舌談哲學

掛墊總是準備禱告

帶著這一切熱情

疲勞的神聖笑聲

是母親在笑。

譯自 *Sinan Antoon* 英譯本

❽ 逝去歲月如死亡

可憐的孤兒呀，沒有揮手說再見。

歲月點點頭走啦，卻不欲消失。

看呀，新年又來到，正解開鞋帶。

毫不留情想要在我們胸前坐365天。

歡迎呀，新年。

我們知道，有時你會以愛與溫柔降臨人間。

通常你卻贈送我們戰爭和悲傷，我們完全瞭解！

即使這樣，我們對你說，歡迎呀，親愛的客人。

帶著你的殘忍、你的溫柔，融入我們當中。

不管發生什麼事，我們永遠不會對你生氣、離棄你。

所以，歡迎！歡迎！

一年過去，又一年來到。

我們時代沒有原罪，不會重返死亡。

那麼，世界呀，新年快樂！

老是把我們的夢想墮胎殺害的世界呀！

譯自 Mohammad Helmi Rishah 英譯本

❾ 讚美父親

我的父親，穿著輕鬆褲子

襯衫沾著泥土氣息

他頭額寬如麥田

眼睛注視愛情

仰望綠色橄欖樹

用思慕的糖果

測量哈迪德*與波昂的距離

那地名他心中有數

他依舊心潮澎湃

像阿夫林河**

艱險、頑強又粗暴

他只畏懼神

也怕與另一兒子

分離

他依舊每天

以他的破阿拉伯語

用念珠

重複祈求五次

一再跪拜

向神請求千次

保護孩子免受傷害

他依舊

只向客人

以及祈禱者

還有小果園裡的幼苗鞠躬

如此而已

他依舊坐在

院子裡的

木椅上

自豪地跟客人說話

自豪地傾聽

自豪地沉默

自豪地笑著

自豪地與遠方

很遠的地平線

握手

…………

…………

但是，當他每天

在永不離身的

舊收音機上

聽新聞時

皺紋和幾十年悲傷

侵犯他的相貌

他喃喃低語：

人，依舊那麼美好！

*謝赫‧哈迪德（Shaykh al-Hadid），敘利亞北方小鎮。
**阿夫林河（Afrin），是奧龍特斯河（orontes river）在
　土耳其和敘利亞境內的支流。

譯自 *Sinan Antoon* 英譯本

❿ 庫德斯坦

在我心房的陽台上

血滴挺立警戒

像受傷母獅

而一朵悲傷嘴唇的百合

冒出地面。

我的血隨心跳同聲往下淌

抱著百合悲傷的臉

嘴唇變成紫色：

在此，誕生家園：庫德斯坦。

譯自 *Norddine Zouitni* 英譯本

⑪ 螞蟻的鞋子

1
麻雀緊張喳喳叫
恐怖的太陽
毒蛇大鬧窩巢
小雞群呼救。

2
有些蟲吃樹幹
其他蟲忙於織絲線。

3
凌晨
人睡著了

水仙花芳香

填補空間。

4

樹葉揮霍灑落

秋天呼出最後一口氣。

5

地球哭出聲

哀叫蓋過我的呻吟

混蛋，你對她幹什麼？

6

高山上的湖泊

好奇的雲雀想不通

水怎能爬到如此險峻高度？

7

湖面上

母鴨帶著小鴨子

母獅瞪著她說：

她確實值得當領導者！

8

野花在河邊生長

蝴蝶從花唇吸花蜜

河水永遠暢流

花蜜用不完

9
在綠色田野

牛咀嚼草

兒童賴牛奶成長

土壤賴糞肥沃。

10
他視魚為長期伙伴

他是真正水手。

11

蜻蜓飛離黃蜂

躲在洞裡

幸運的是黃蜂！

12

狐狸正在磨牙

笨母雞還在偏僻逛。

13

微風吹過

說我是風的嬌女

14

他買褲子不要口袋

他知道根本用不上！

15

螞蟻的鞋子很小，

小到無論走到哪裡

地面總保持乾淨。

16

春天在大地散發芬芳

麻雀笑說

神的恩賜真可愛！

17

龜裂的山

永遠不會滾下來

只會變成礫石。

18

快要坍塌的房子裡

石頭不會碎

蓋房子的人心會。

19

爸爸問公雞：你為什麼會報曉？

公雞答：只是父傳子的習慣。

20

狐狸心跳

衝著雞的咯咯叫聲。

譯自 Norddine Zouitni 英譯本

⑫ 虎

小時候

想成為有強爪的老虎

可以攻擊擋路的人。

長大時，想成為環遊世界的

老虎，不要爪。

年老時

想成為單純老虎，

或是有房子和屋頂的

老虎

保護自己免受虎爪傷害。

譯自 *Margaret Saine* 英譯本

⓭ 哭泣

她早上哭

她中午哭

她晚上哭

早上她失去一個兒子

中午她又失去另一個

晚上她失去最後一個

第二天早上他們為她哭

中午他們為哭她的人而哭

晚上沒剩下哭聲

全鎮血流遍地。

譯自 Mony Zinati 英譯本

⑭ 四棵樹

他們砍伐四棵樹

他們用第一棵製作搖籃

他們用第二棵製作情人床

他們用第三棵製作老人枴杖

他們用第四棵製作王宮椅子

儘管貧窮，第一、第二和第三棵樹都很高興

儘管王宮說不盡富麗堂皇

第四棵樹很是悲傷

譯自 *Mony Zinati* 英譯本

⓯ 母親的辛勞

門愛窗戶

窗戶愛椅子

椅子愛桌子

樹喜歡說：謝天謝地

我為孩子的一切辛勞和吃苦

沒有白費！

譯自 Mony Zinati 英譯本

⓰ 微笑的綠樹

一棵樹

始終翠綠帶笑容

有人想要知道祕密

打開樹心

找到一隻鳥

在動脈之際飛翔

在中間築巢。

譯自 *Mony Zinati* 英譯本

⓱ 有何不可？

桌子想成為椅子

椅子說：有何不可？

我老是希望有一個妹妹。

譯自 Mony Zinati 英譯本

⑱ 妒忌

灌木對喬木說：

已經夠了吧

不管你長多高

頭永遠搆不到天空

喬木俯身對灌木

低語：

嫉妒夠了吧

夠了吧。

譯自 *Mony Zinati* 英譯本

⑲ 雨傘

樹看到兩位裸身孩子

在雨中寒顫

就跑

向他們快跑

張開樹葉

站在他們上方

像一把雨傘。

譯自 Mony Zinati 英譯本

❷⓿ 樹的夢想

樹在夢中，看到自己飛翔

群鳥清早來造訪樹

贈送羽毛和翅膀

要樹一同飛翔。

譯自 Mony Zinati 英譯本

㉑ 樹和項鍊

樹想要在長頸上掛金項鍊

群鳥在此地聚集

彼此並行排列

溫暖裝飾樹的長頸。

譯自 Mony Zinati 英譯本

㉒ 兩棵樹

　　有兩位情人坐在下方
　　樹笑臉燦爛
　　有蛇住在軀幹內
　　樹始終臉色愴然。

譯自 Mony Zinati 英譯本

❷❸ 垂柳

他們問垂柳

為什麼總是這樣喪氣？

出乎意外回答：不，我不喪氣

但為什麼枝葉總是淚水垂滴？

柳樹笑著說

不是你想像的那樣

我是剛剛洗完澡。

譯自 *Mony Zinati* 英譯本

㉔ 木炭

樹說：

如果他們折斷以自由名義寫作的所有鉛筆

我會焚燒我的一根樹枝

燒成木炭，做粉筆！

在世界所有牆壁自由書寫：

「自由萬歲！」

譯自 *Mony Zinati* 英譯本

㉕ 樹的悲哀

樹在傷心

灰塵沾滿綠葉

雨遲遲不下

天呀

你太吝嗇啦！

譯自 *Mony Zinati* 英譯本

㉖ 我但願是

樹被鋸斷

他們用蘆葦製作長笛

樹說：

我但願是一根蘆葦。

譯自 *Mony Zinati* 英譯本

㉗ 競賽

白楊告訴柏樹：

因為我們頭永遠無法到達天庭

與其這種無意義競賽

不如彼此擁抱吧

譯自 Mony Zinati 英譯本

㉘ 勇氣

突然
樹抽掉斧頭手柄
說：這是我的一部分
不想成為敵人幫手！

譯自 *Mony Zinati* 英譯本

㉙ 棺材

他們用樹木製造棺材時
是多麼痛苦
多麼傷心
但是棺材內躺著烈士時
有了得意的笑容
感到大為自豪。

譯自 Mony Zinati 英譯本

㉚ 慈悲

　　鳥築巢

　　在高大樹上

　　樹求神

　　我祈求祢

　　不要往這方向送暴風雨。

　　　　　　　　　　　　譯自 *Mony Zinati* 英譯本

㉛ 樹和將軍

一位卑鄙將軍

從戰場回來

想在樹下休息

樹命令所有的鳥

聚在一起滴屎

到罪惡將軍頭上！

譯自 Mony Zinati 英譯本

㉜ 失望

樹因下雨大為失望

喊叫：神呀，我要一把雨傘！

譯自 *Mony Zinati* 英譯本

㉝ 禮品

夜夜寂寞時

他爬到屋頂上

摘星星

逐一

串成光亮項鍊

早上

獻給妳。

譯自 *Mony Zinati* 英譯本

㉞ 如果你遇到傷心女

如果你遇到傷心女

請勿說「神與妳同在」

請勿說「神助妳紓解悲傷」

不，不

不要對她說這些

以溫暖的心擁抱她

對她輕聲細語

妳是世界上最美的女人

妳的眼睛比所有女人的眼睛都要美

當妳微笑時

妳如花笑容處處開心

然後妳會看到

愛情的眼睛重新閃亮

精神多麼煥發

多麼快就會忘掉悲傷。

譯自 *Mony Zinati* 英譯本

㉟ 健忘

當薰衣草眼見飢餓

傷心說

但願我是麥田

森林樹木聽到就說

希望我們的果實是小麥

雨也聽到，就說

希望我的雨滴變成小麥

滴入餓肚子裡

泥巴也聽到，就說

希望我全部都變成小麥

連石頭聽到都說

希望我們的心變成小麥

只有人聽到時說

我但願……

卻忘了完成句子！

譯自 *Mony Zinati* 英譯本

㊱ 拉雪茲神父公墓

我在拉雪茲神父公墓

看到一位死者。

我只看見

高大的墳墓

抬頭向

天空

有一隻小松鼠

在巴爾扎克肩上竄動

用敏銳耳朵聽

悲傷歌聲

來自

琵雅芙家族墓。

霎時，我以為是

聽到伊迪絲・琵雅芙*在呻吟。

*伊迪絲・琵雅芙（Edith Piaf），法國國寶級女歌手，電影《玫瑰人生》（La Môme）即演其一生故事。

譯自 *Allison Blecker* 英譯本

㊲ 阿夫林*

我心目中的天國

阿夫林呀，神在大自然面前最後的精湛球技

在頑固山脈胸部下方生長的彩色鬱金香

從傳說眼中掉落的石碑

雲雀、鴿子和松雞嘴上的甜言蜜語……

阿夫林呀，庫爾德人寵壞的瞪羚

被橄欖樹、漆樹、麥穗和葡萄園的笑聲捲曲的毛髮

女人睡在情人床上，而她的辮子被嘶嘶毒蛇和暴

　　君一時興起所污。

阿夫林呀，泥屋被覆指甲花、葡萄乾和祖母的睫毛

用祖先語言所寫的故事和傳說，充滿回憶和渴望。

阿夫林呀，政治家、空談家、騙子和叛徒口中的
　　瑣事。
阿夫林呀，像指環繞著地球的海洋
用前臂寫的記錄
鳳凰用喙指向四面八方
且說：那些是我們的心、
我們人民修詞的邊界
那些是我們的愛、永恆愛的極限。

　　　　*阿夫林是敘利亞的古城，位於該國西北部。

　　　　　　　　　　　　　　　　譯自 *Norddine Zouitni* 英譯本

關於詩人

　　胡塞殷・哈巴實（Hussein Habasch），1970年出
生於庫德斯坦，現住在德國波昂，以庫德文和阿拉伯
文寫作。部分詩作被譯成英文、德文、西班牙文、法
文、土耳其文、波斯文、烏茲別克文、俄文和羅馬尼
亞文，並被選入多種國際詩選。出版詩集有《沉溺於
玫瑰》（2002年）、《逃亡越過埃夫羅斯河》（2004
年）、《比慾望高且比瞪羚腰肉美味》（2007年）、
《對薩利姆・巴拉卡特迷惑》（2009年）、《飛行天

使》（2013年）、西班牙文《不通過》（2016年）、
羅馬尼亞文《有廚師的樹》（2017年）、西班牙文
《兩棵樹》（2017年）等。參加過哥倫比亞、尼加拉
瓜、法國、波多黎各、墨西哥、德國、羅馬尼亞、立
陶宛、摩洛哥、厄瓜多、薩爾瓦多、科索沃、哥斯達
黎加、保加利亞、馬其頓等國際詩歌節，2019年來台
灣參加淡水福爾摩莎國際詩歌節。

關於漢語譯者

　　李魁賢，1937年生，1953年開始發表詩作，曾任台灣筆會會長，國家文化藝術基金會董事長。現任世界詩人運動組織（Movimiento Poetas del Mundo）副會長。詩被譯成各種語文在日本、韓國、加拿大、紐西蘭、荷蘭、南斯拉夫、羅馬尼亞、印度、希臘、美國、西班牙、巴西、蒙古、俄羅斯、古巴、智利、尼加拉瓜、孟加拉、馬其頓、土耳其、波蘭等國發表。

　　出版著作包括《李魁賢詩集》全6冊、《李魁賢文集》全10冊、《李魁賢譯詩集》全8冊、翻譯《歐洲經典詩選》全25冊、《名流詩叢》34冊、《人生拼圖─李魁賢回憶錄》，及其他共二百本。英譯詩集有《愛是我的信仰》、《溫柔的美感》、《島與島之間》、《黃昏時刻》和《存在或不存在》。《黃昏時刻》共有英文、蒙古文、羅馬尼亞文、俄文、西班牙文、法文、韓文、孟加拉文、阿爾巴尼亞文和土耳其文譯本。

曾獲韓國亞洲詩人貢獻獎、榮後台灣詩獎、賴和文學獎、行政院文化獎、印度麥氏學會詩人獎、吳三連獎新詩獎、台灣新文學貢獻獎、蒙古文化基金會文化名人獎牌和詩人獎章、蒙古建國八百週年成吉思汗金牌、成吉思汗大學金質獎章和蒙古作家聯盟推廣蒙古文學貢獻獎、真理大學台灣文學家牛津獎、韓國高麗文學獎、孟加拉卡塔克文學獎、馬其頓奈姆·弗拉舍里文學獎。

❶*The red snow*

The snow comes down white

Covering all the mountains with whiteness

The snow comes down white on Kurdistan's

mountains too

But it soon become red.

Translated by Muna Zinati

❷ *Just Know That I Died*

If one day you came and did not find me

Just know I am there

If you came there and did not find me

Just know I am in a faraway place

If you came that far and do not find me

Do not be sad

Plant a red rose deep in the heart of the earth

And know that I died!

Translated by Muna Zinati

❸ *The Use of Love*

All know the earth is round

No doubt it rotates

But they do not know

That the Lovers heart is what makes it round

And the strength of their love

What makes it rotate.

Translated by Muna Zinati

❹ *The Love of Two Trees*

Two trees were madly in love

The vindictive woodchopper

Cuts their trunks off

He took them home

By chance the two trees met in the fire place

They embraced happily

And burned together.

Translated by Muna Zinati

❺ *Tomorrow You Will Be an Old Man*

(For me, in a quarter of a century, more or less)

Tomorrow you will be an old man

The cane always with you

You will walk alone

You will mutter to yourself like all old geezers do

You will become obstinate, hard of hearing, and slow

You will ask for help when you need it

and no one will respond

You will dream of the past

and the good old days

While your grandson will think of the future

and days to come

You will curse this vapid generation

Repeating like a broken record

How wonderful our generation was

You will be the butt of jokes in the family

They will laugh at you and your positions

which you think are right on

Your lips will let a sarcastic smile

whenever they mention words like stubbornness,

vigor, and faith in the future

You might even laugh

Your bones will soften

Sicknesses will roam freely in your body

without permission

All your desires will be extinguished

except the desire to die

There will be no friend or companion

Loneliness will be your support and comrade

You will always be ready to depart

The threshold of the grave will entice you and keep

    you company

All the angels will betray you and leave

Only Azrael will approach you as a last friend

Perhaps you will say just as you are about to go:

If I die, burry me here in the strangers' cemetery

Perhaps these words

will be you your final wish.

Translated by Sinan Antoon

❻ *Beethoven and Kurds*

I look at Beethoven's figure

He appears sad

Crowds of Kurds

inspect the city center with their steps

Nothing dwells in them except longing

Beethoven cries

I look at the Rhine

cleaving the city into two

It appears sad

Is it sad for the Euphrates?

The Euphrates is sad.

Translated by Sinan Antoon

❼ *My Mother's Chants*

1. The Vision Chant

This morning, my mother was sitting alone at home

Mending my brother Mahmoud's pants

Torn by yesterday's mischief

The needle pierced her finger and warm blood flowed

    on the thread

The pants were stained and my mother's thoughts

    were muddled

She swore to my father and the neighbors

that she saw me or my shadow

Or saw me without my shadow passing before her this

morning

And when she saw me

she was so eager she was confused and was about to

hug me

But the needle betrayed her and pierced her finger

Was I really there

or was it my mother's heart?

2.　The Longing Chant

Mother,

Thirty years and I am still running with a barefoot heart

Whenever I see a woman wearing a long dress

Or a white scarf on her head

I call out to her: Mother, mother

Mother!

Thirty years and six thousand miles

Exiled from roses, morning sunrise, and the face of

　　angels,

mother's face

Thirty years

Whenever I write about a woman

Whenever I draw a woman

I find myself writing about my mother

clothing the image with my mother's colors

Thirty shrouds, thirty graves, thirty . . .

I treat with hope and peace of mind

Whenever I lay my head

on my mother's chest.

3.   The Passion Chant

The inscriptions on the walls of our mud house

The yellow paint on the door

The family picture carefully hung next to Imam Ali's

The traces of a tattoo on the baking tin

The big quiet stone next to the door

Always ready to receive guests

Shelves crowded with old newspapers

The lamp philosophizing with a long luminous tongue

The hanging mat always ready for prayer

The sacred laugh that brought all this passion

and this weariness

is my mother's laugh.

Translated by Sinan Antoon

❽ *Years Gone Like Death*

Without waving its hand and saying goodbye, O poor
orphans.

The year nodded its head and went without desire to
extinguish.

Behold, a new year has come, and behold, it opens its
shoelace.

And would like to sit on our chest for 365 days without
mercy.

Welcome New Year.

We know that sometimes you will fall upon us with
love and tenderness.

And usually you gift us wars and grief, we know this
completely!

But even so, we will say to you, welcome, dear guest.

With your cruelty, your softness, you are among us.

No matter what happens, we will never be mad on
  you and leave you.

So, welcome, welcome.

A year gone, a year comes.

And our age goes without sin, without returning to its
  death.

A Happy New Year, then, O World.

O world that aborts our dreams and kills them always!

Translated by Mohammad Helmi Rishah

❾ *In Praise of my Father*

My father, his trousers flowing

His shirt adorned with the scent of earth

His forehead wide as a field of wheat

is still gazing with eyes of love and longing

at the green olive trees

Measuring, with the sugar of yearning,

the distance between Shaykh al-Hadid and Bonn

whose name he knows by heart

He is still surging

like the river Afrin

hard, stubborn, and rough

He only fears God

and separation

from another son

He is still repeating his supplications

in his broken Arabic

on the prayer beads

five times every day

Asking God a thousand times

between one bow and another

to protect his children from harm

He is still simple

bowing to guests,

prayer,

and the seedlings in his little orchard

but nothing else

He is still sitting

on his wooden chair

in the courtyard

speaking to his guests with pride

listening with pride

silent with pride

laughing with pride

shaking hands with the distant,

very distant, horizon,

with pride

He is still comparing

butterflies and humans

trees and humans

love and humans

the sun and humans

earth and humans

. . . .

. . . .

But when he listens

to the news every day

on his old radio

which never leaves his side

wrinkles and decades of sorrow

invade his features

He mutters:

still, humans are so beautiful!

Translated by Sinan Antoon

⑩ *Kurdistan*

On the veranda of my heart

Blood drops stood alert

Like wounded lionesses

While out of the earth

A lily with sad lips sprang up.

Down ran my blood in unison with my heartbeats

It hugged the sad face of the lily

Turning its lips purple :

There, a homeland was born: Kurdistan.

Translated by Norddine Zouitni

⑪ *The Ant's shoes*

1

Sparrows chirp nervously

A fearful sun

The viper messes up with the nests

The chicks cry out for help.

2

Worms eat into tree trunks

Other worms weave silk threads.

3

Early morning

People asleep

The fragrant scent of daffodils

fills up space.

4

Leaves falling off profusely

Autumn is giving up its last breath.

5

Earth is crying out

Her shouts drown out my moaning

What did you, villains, do to Her?

6

A lake on top of a high mountain

The amazed lark wonders

How did water climb to such rugged height?

7

On the face of the lake

The duck leads its young

The lioness gazes at her and says:

She's worthy of leadership indeed!

8

A wild flower grew on the river's edge

A butterfly sucks the nectar from the flower's lips

The river flows forever

The nectar won't run out

9

In the green fields

The cow chews grass

Milk for kids' growth

Dung for soil fertility.

10

He named the fish a longtime companion

He was a real sailor.

11

The dragonfly runs away from wasps

And hides inside their hole

So fortunate are the wasps!

12

The fox grinds his teeth

The foolish hen is round the corner.

13

A small breeze blew

And said I am the wind's spoilt daughter.

14

He bought pants without pockets

He knows he doesn't need them at all!

15

The ant's shoes are tiny, so tiny

That wherever she treads

The ground stays clean.

16

Spring spreads out its fragrance over earth

The sparow laughs

And says: so lovely are God's gifts !

17

The cracked mountain

Will never roll down

It will turn into rubble.

18

In the house about to fall

The stones won't crumple in

But the hearts of those that built it will.

19

My dad asks the rooster: Why do you crow?

The rooster anwers: just a habit passed down from

father to son.

20

The fox's hearbeats point

Towards chikens' cackling.

Translated by Norddine Zouitni

⓬ *Tiger*

When I was young

I wanted to be a tiger with strong claws

to attack anyone who would block my path.

When I grew up, I wanted to be a tiger

who would travel around the world, without claws.

When I got old

I wanted to be just a tiger,

or a tiger

who has a house and a roof

to protect himself from the claws of tigers.

Translated by Margaret Saine

⓭ *Weeping*

She wept in the morning

She wept at noon

She wept in the evening

At morning she lost a son

At noon she lost another

At evening she lost the last of the bunch

In the next morning they cried for her

At noon they cried for whom were crying for her

At evening there was no remaining cries

The whole town was swamped with blood.

Translated by Mony Zinati

⓲ *Four trees*

They cut four trees

They made a cradle from the first one

They made a lover's bed from the second one

They made a cane for an old man from the third one

They made a chair for the king's palace from the
  fourth one

Despite the poverty, the first, second and third trees
  were very happy

Despite the wealth and the beauty of the king's palace

The forth tree was very sad.

Translated by Mony Zinati

⑮ *Mother's Effort*

The door loved the window

The window loved the chair

The chair loved the table

The tree happily said: Thank God

All my efforts and toil for my children

Were not in vain!

Translated by Mony Zinati

⓰ *A Smiling Green Tree*

A tree

Was always green and smily

They wanted to know her secret

They opened its heart

Found a bird

Flying from one artery to another

Building his nest in the middle.

Translated by Mony Zinati

⑰ *Why not?*

A table wanted to become a chair

The chair said: Why not?

I always wished I had a sister.

Translated by Mony Zinati

⓲ *Jealousy*

The short tree told the long tree:

Enough already

No matter how high you get

Your head will never reach the sky

The long tree bent over the short tree

Whispered to her:

Enough jealousy

Enough.

Translated by Mony Zinati

⑲ *Umbrella*

The tree saw two nearly naked children

In the rain shivering from the cold

It ran

It ran fast toward them

Opened its leaves

Stood above them

Like an umbrella.

Translated by Mony Zinati

⓴ *A tree's dream*

In a dream a tree saw itself fly

All birds visited the tree in the morning

They gifted it feathers and wings

And made it fly with them.

Translated by Mony Zinati

㉑ *The tree and the necklace*

A tree wanted a golden necklace for its long neck

The birds at that place met together

They lined beside each other

Warmly decorated the tree's long neck.

Translated by Mony Zinati

㉒ *Two trees*

The tree under which the two lovers sat underneath

Had a bright smiling face

The tree in whose trunk the snake lived

Had always a pale sad face.

Translated by Mony Zinati

㉓ *The Weeping Willow*

They asked the weeping willow

Why are you always sad like that?

Surprisingly it answered: No I am not sad

But why are your twigs and leafs always hanging and

    dripping tears?

The willow tree laughed and said

It's not as you imagine

It's just that I took a bath.

Translated by Mony Zinati

㉔ *Charcoal*

A tree said:

If they broke all the pencils which wrote in the name

   of freedom

I will burn one of my branches

Make it charcoal, chalk!

For the free to write on all the world's walls:

"Long Live Freedom"

Translated by Mony Zinati

㉕ *A Tree's Grief*

A tree was sad

The dust occupied its greenish leaves

The rainfall was delayed

Oh heaven

You are so stingy!

Translated by Mony Zinati

❷❻ *I Wish I*

When a tree saw

They make flutes from the reeds

It said:

I wish I were a reed.

Translated by Mony Zinati

Race

The poplar tree told the cypress tree:

Since our heads will never reach heaven

Instead of this pointless race

Let's hug each other.

Translated by Mony Zinati

㉘ *Bravery*

Suddenly

The tree extracted the axe's handle

And said: This is a part of me

I do not want it to be a help to my enemy!

Translated by Mony Zinati

㉙ *Coffin*

When they made a coffin out of the tree

It had so much pain

And was so saddened

But when they lay the martyr inside it

It had a wonderful smile

And felt a great pride.

Translated by Mony Zinati

30 *Mercy*

A bird built his nest

Atop a high tree

The tree called God

I beg you God

Do not send storms in my direction.

Translated by Mony Zinati

㉛ *The Tree and the General*

A dirty General

Was back from war

He wanted to rest under the tree

The tree ordered all its birds

To drip all together

On top of the criminal general's head!

Translated by Mony Zinati

㉜ *Disappointment*

A tree was disappointed at the rain

It called: Oh God, I want an umbrella!

Translated by Mony Zinati

㉝ *Gift*

Each night in his loneliness

On top of his roof

He plucks up the stars from the sky

One by one

Makes a luminous necklace

In the morning

He offers it to you.

Translated by Mony Zinati

34 *If you ever come across a sad woman*

If you ever come across a sad woman

Do not say "God be with you"

Do not say: God help you relieve your grief

No... No

Do not tell her all that

Embrace her with a warm heart

Whisper to her

You are the most beautiful woman in the world

Your eyes are more beautiful than all women's eyes

When you smile

Your flowery smile will open up everywhere

Then you will see

How love will shine through her eyes again

How her spirit will thrive

And how fast she will forget her sorrows.

Translated by Mony Zinati

35 *Forgetfulness*

When a spike saw the hungry through her eye

It was so sad and said

I wish I were a wheat field

The forest trees heard it and said

We wish our fruits were wheat

The rain also heard it and said

I wish my rain drops become wheat

Dripping through hungry bellies

The dirt heard it too and said

I wish the whole of me became wheat

Even the stones when they heard it said

We wish our hearts become wheat

Only the human heard it and said

I wish.......

But he forgot to finish his sentence!

Translated by Mony Zinati

㊱ *Père Lachaise Cemetery*

I saw one dead person,

in Père Lachaise Cemetery.

I saw only

lofty tombs

raising their heads

to the sky

and a small squirrel

worrying Balzac's shoulder

and listening with sharp ears

to the sorrowful singing

coming from

the Piaf family tomb.

For a moment, I thought

I heard Edith Piaf moaning.

Translated by Allison Blecker

❸❼ *Afrin*

The city of God over my heart's shoulder

Afrin, God's last masterful kick in the face of nature

A colorful tulip grown under the breasts of stubborn
   mountains

A stone tablet fallen from the eyes of legends

Sweet words on the lips of skylarks, pigeonsa and
   grouses······

Afrin, the spoilt Gazelle of Kurds

Whose hair is plaited with the laughter of olive trees,
   sumac, wheat ears, and vineyards

A woman asleep in her lover's bed while her plaits
   are being defiled by hissing vipers
   and whims of tyrants.

Afrin, mud houses coated with henna, raisins and
    grandmothers' eyelashes
A story and legend written in the ancestors' language
    heavy with memories and longing.
Afrin, a trifle in the mouths of politicians, pedants,
    dodgers, and renegades.
Afrin, an ocean surrounding earth like a ring
A record written with the forearm
The Phoenix points its beak in all directions
And says: Those are the borders of our hearts,
The rhetoric of our people
Those are the frontiers of our love, our everlasting love.

Translated by Norddine Zouitni

Contents

語言文學類　PG2225　名流詩叢34

紅雪
The Red Snow

原　　著 / 胡塞殷・哈巴實（Hussein Habash）
譯　　者 / 李魁賢（Lee Kuei-shien）
責任編輯 / 林昕平
圖文排版 / 林宛榆
封面設計 / 蔡瑋筠

發 行 人 / 宋政坤
法律顧問 / 毛國樑　律師
出版發行 / 秀威資訊科技股份有限公司
　　　　　114台北市內湖區瑞光路76巷65號1樓
　　　　　電話：+886-2-2796-3638　傳真：+886-2-2796-1377
　　　　　http://www.showwe.com.tw
劃撥帳號 / 19563868　戶名：秀威資訊科技股份有限公司
　　　　　讀者服務信箱：service@showwe.com.tw
展售門市 / 國家書店（松江門市）
　　　　　104台北市中山區松江路209號1樓
　　　　　電話：+886-2-2518-0207　傳真：+886-2-2518-0778
網路訂購 / 秀威網路書店：https://store.showwe.tw
　　　　　國家網路書店：https://www.govbooks.com.tw

2019年8月　BOD一版
定價：200元
版權所有　翻印必究
本書如有缺頁、破損或裝訂錯誤，請寄回更換

國家圖書館出版品預行編目

紅雪 / 胡塞殷.哈巴實(Hussein Habash)著 ; 李
魁賢(Lee Kuei-shien)譯. -- 一版. -- 臺北市 :
秀威資訊科技, 2019.08
　　面 ；　公分. -- (語言文學類. 名流詩叢 ;
34)
　　中英對照
　　BOD版
　　譯自 : The Red Snow
　　ISBN 978-986-326-714-0(平裝)

864.551　　　　　　　　　　　108011056

讀 者 回 函 卡

感謝您購買本書，為提升服務品質，請填妥以下資料，將讀者回函卡直接寄回或傳真本公司，收到您的寶貴意見後，我們會收藏記錄及檢討，謝謝！
如您需要了解本公司最新出版書目、購書優惠或企劃活動，歡迎您上網查詢或下載相關資料：http:// www.showwe.com.tw

您購買的書名：＿＿＿＿＿＿＿＿＿＿＿＿＿＿＿＿＿＿＿＿＿＿＿

出生日期：＿＿＿＿＿年＿＿＿＿＿月＿＿＿＿＿日

學歷：□高中 (含) 以下　　□大專　　□研究所 (含) 以上

職業：□製造業　□金融業　□資訊業　□軍警　□傳播業　□自由業
　　　□服務業　□公務員　□教職　　□學生　□家管　　□其它＿＿＿

購書地點：□網路書店　□實體書店　□書展　□郵購　□贈閱　□其他

您從何得知本書的消息？

　□網路書店　□實體書店　□網路搜尋　□電子報　□書訊　□雜誌
　□傳播媒體　□親友推薦　□網站推薦　□部落格　□其他＿＿＿＿＿

您對本書的評價：(請填代號　1.非常滿意　2.滿意　3.尚可　4.再改進)

　封面設計＿＿＿　版面編排＿＿＿　內容＿＿＿　文／譯筆＿＿＿　價格＿＿＿

讀完書後您覺得：

　□很有收穫　□有收穫　□收穫不多　□沒收穫

對我們的建議：＿＿＿＿＿＿＿＿＿＿＿＿＿＿＿＿＿＿＿＿＿＿＿
＿＿＿＿＿＿＿＿＿＿＿＿＿＿＿＿＿＿＿＿＿＿＿＿＿＿＿＿＿＿＿
＿＿＿＿＿＿＿＿＿＿＿＿＿＿＿＿＿＿＿＿＿＿＿＿＿＿＿＿＿＿＿
＿＿＿＿＿＿＿＿＿＿＿＿＿＿＿＿＿＿＿＿＿＿＿＿＿＿＿＿＿＿＿

11466
台北市內湖區瑞光路 76 巷 65 號 1 樓
秀威資訊科技股份有限公司　　　收
BOD 數位出版事業部

....

（請沿線對折寄回，謝謝！）

姓　　名：＿＿＿＿＿＿＿＿＿　年齡：＿＿＿＿　性別：□女　□男

郵遞區號：□□□□□

地　　址：＿＿＿＿＿＿＿＿＿＿＿＿＿＿＿＿＿＿＿＿＿＿＿

聯絡電話：(日)＿＿＿＿＿＿＿＿＿＿＿(夜)＿＿＿＿＿＿＿＿＿＿＿

E-mail：＿＿＿＿＿＿＿＿＿＿＿＿＿＿＿＿＿＿＿＿＿＿＿